Sister Anita Parks

W9-AOB-073

For Norma and Clarry

First U.S. edition 1994
Text and illustrations copyright © 1994 by Dave and Julie Saunders
The Big Storm copyright © 1994 by Frances Lincoln Limited

Bradbury Press
Macmillan Publishing Company
866 Third Avenue
New York, NY 10022

Macmillan Publishing Company is part of the
Maxwell Communication Group of Companies.

First published in Great Britain in 1994, with the title *The Big Storm*,
by Frances Lincoln Limited, 4 Torriano Mews, Torriano Avenue,
London NW5 2RZ

Printed and bound in Italy
10 9 8 7 6 5 4 3 2 1

Library of Congress Catalog Card Number 93-074922

ISBN 0-02-778134-8

STORM'S COMING

Dave and Julie Saunders

Bradbury Press   New York

It was a crisp autumn day, and the Squirrels were out looking for nuts.

They looked and nibbled, until they were far away from their comfortable home in the hollow of the old oak tree.

In the clearing they met Fox. He was worried.

"Hide and shelter," he barked. "There's a storm coming, Squirrels — and I'm going to my den to keep dry."

By the mossy bank they met Badger. He was in a hurry.

"Hide and shelter," he growled. "There's a storm coming, Squirrels — and I'm going to my sett to keep dry."

Out on the hillside they saw the Rabbits. They looked twitchy.

"Hide and shelter," they snuffled. "There's a storm coming, Squirrels — and we're going to our burrows to keep dry."

On his way home to his nest, Mouse felt the first drops of rain and hid himself under the biggest leaf he could find.

"Must keep dry," he squeaked.

Owl peered anxiously out over the darkening wood.

"Hide and shelter, everyone!" he shrieked. "Here comes the storm!"

At last the pounding rain fell more gently, turning into a soft drizzle. Badger and the Rabbits peeked out from their homes.

"Look how deep the puddles are!" said Badger.

Fox and Mouse saw the first patch of blue sky.
"Hurray," said Fox, "the storm is passing!"

When the sun broke through, Owl, the Rabbits, Fox, Mouse, and Badger gathered in the clearing.

"We're safe!" they all cried. "But where are the Squirrels?"

Two muffled voices called out from a hollow log.
"Here we are! We're in here!" the Squirrels
chorused.

The other animals gathered round and stared.
What *were* the Squirrels doing still hiding in there?

"Look what we've found
in *our* shelter,"
squeaked the Squirrels.
"Nuts! Lots of them."
    And while the Squirrels
munched their feast,
the other animals
basked in the warm sun.
    The big storm was over!